PRODOMON—

BRINGER OF FEAR

PRODOMON—

BRINGER OF FEAR

VICTORIA NOLAN

authorHOUSE®

AuthorHouse™
1663 Liberty Drive
Bloomington, IN 47403
www.authorhouse.com
Phone: 1-800-839-8640

First published by AuthorHouse   01/26/2012

ISBN: 978-1-4685-4864-8 (sc)
ISBN: 978-1-4685-4865-5 (ebk)

Library of Congress Control Number: 2012901680

Printed in the United States of America

Any people depicted in stock imagery provided by Thinkstock are models, and such images are being used for illustrative purposes only.
Certain stock imagery © Thinkstock.

This book is printed on acid-free paper.

This book is dedicated to my papa for supporting and encouraging me to live my dreams and to my third grade teacher, Mrs. Mooney, who persuaded me to publish this.

PROLOGUE
Sometime in the Future

OUR EPIC BATTLE leaves the last of human kind living in a cave. The battle between the humans and gods had started long before anyone in the cave was born, and time was running out.

It had all started because the gods believed that the humans had become too powerful. The gods asked the God of Science, Hypaneous, to create a monster so powerful that it would be impossible for any human to destroy it. But that was before Daryous was born. Hopefully with him, will the last of the humans survive?

CHAPTER ONE

SITTING AND FREEZING in a cave, fighting for survival, Daryous moved his numb shaky hands towards the fire, his teeth chattering from the cold.

"Ww when i i is it going t to warm u u up in here?" Daryous said aloud still chattering while looking around at the dark dank cave he called home.

He had been hiding in the cave for what seemed like years but there was no real way of knowing how long. Time seemed endless. You see, living was very hard in these times for there was one powerful monster around. His name? Nobody knew for they were sure that they would be destroyed by him before they even saw him! He was so powerful because he was created by the gods! One god in particular, the all powerful God of Science,

Hypaneous. After all, it was his design. He had sculpted the monster out of all the negativity in the world from humans. Then Hypaneous took his brain and life potions, mixed them and poured them into the monster to make him smart and invincible. The monster had the ability to destroy anything or anyone who gets in his way in the name of the gods. Hypaneous then named him Prodomon, bringer of fear. So now the remaining humans in the world are in danger and killing this enemy will not be easy!

As Daryous sat trying to warm himself in the cave, he heard a loud thud outside. "No . . . it can't be . . . how could he find me so . . .", before he had a chance to finish his thought, the roof of the cave started to crumble down.

Prodomon's enormous foot was pushing down on the roof of the cave. Daryous screamed as the roof started to collapse on top of him. He was trapped. He looked up just in time to see Prodomon's foot coming down to crush him.

Chapter Two

Daryous couldn't move. He could only stare in horror as Prodomon's foot was crushing the cave onto him. He rolled out of the way just as Prodomon's foot went through the roof and hit the ground where he was sitting. His blue shirt and khaki shorts were now covered in dirt and rocks, and his once blonde hair now was brown with dirt. Just then bits of broken rock fell on him, pinning him to the cave floor. His blue eyes strained to see the monster through the dust cloud that had formed. It was then that he got his first look at this monster. Prodomon was huge, at least 30 feet tall. He had brown hairy fur all over him. He had enormous razor sharp teeth, two big horns on his head and one red eye that was now staring directly at Daryous. Daryous then realized that this monster was half cyclops and half minotaur.

"Oh god, what in the world is this thing?", Daryous thought as he was trying to pull himself out from under the crushed rocks. Just as Prodomon's foot was coming down to try to crush him again, he heard his name.

"Daryous . . . move!", Ginger screamed.

Daryous looked over to see Ginger standing at the edge of the trees just beyond the now crushed cave entrance. Her long blond hair was streaked with dust from the falling rocks and her clothes looked like they had seen many battles. The t shirt she wore, that had been pink, was now gray; and her jeans were ripped through at the knees. Her blue eyes were bloodshot, and tears were forming and running down her face.

"Obviously over me", he thought. She never looked more beautiful to him then just now.

"Run, Daryous run," she screamed.

"What?", he yelled over the falling rocks and growling sound that now was coming from Prodomons mouth.

"Are you crazy, stay back!", Daryous yelled as Ginger was starting to approach the cave.

"Just run . . . I'll take care of him, ok", she said running toward Daryous.

Not fully trusting Ginger, Daryous grabbed a piece of wood that was in the fire and threw it at Prodomon's foot. The torch startled Prodomon long enough for Daryous to pull himself out of the rocks, and run out of the cave just as Ginger entered and started to attack Prodomon with a club she had made out of a tree branch.

As he ran, he questioned if he had done the right thing by leaving Ginger there to defend herself against the monster. He knew if he left, Ginger may get hurt; but if he went back to save her, then he may get eaten. So he left. He knew he had to trust that Ginger would be able to handle herself. She always had in the past when they had encountered other life and death situations.

He figured that she would meet up with him later at their secret place high up in the mountains of what used to be the city of Hollywood. As he ran, he could see the once magical Hollywood sign now smashed to pieces and the remainder of a once beautiful city now in ruins at the bottom of the valley. Some of the buildings still stood around crumpled piles of rubble that were once homes and businesses. What had been a thriving city was now a ghost town and, as far as he knew, Ginger and he were the only humans that had survived. He found the entrance to the tunnel which he thought had once been a house built into the hill, and waited for Ginger to arrive. While he waited, the sky grew dark and the air got cold. Unknowingly, he had fallen asleep. When he woke, the sun was just coming up. He looked around, but Ginger was no where to be found. He ran out of the tunnel to find that she was not outside anywhere either. Realizing that she had not returned from the cave, Daryous began shaking with fear.

"Oh no, what have I done?"

CHAPTER THREE

REGAINING HIS SENSES, Daryous jumped up and ran toward the cave. Finally he arrived at the cave. He stared in horror at the pile of rocks in front of the cave. He saw Ginger lying lifeless beneath the pile of rocks. He dropped to his knees and began to cry.

"Why, why her, why now?" he cried.

They had been through situations like this before and she had always managed to come out of it unharmed somehow. He sat there for a while crying and staring at her body. He tried to imagine what his life would be like without her, and his chest began to ache. Finally he grabbed the rocks and moved them off of Ginger's body. Once she was uncovered, he dragged her out of the cave and into the foggy mist of the morning. He listened for a heartbeat or shallow breath, but there was none. She was gone. He looked around for something to use to dig a hole to bury her in. He found a broken tree limb and started to dig. He dragged Ginger's body to the edge of the hole. He placed a gentle kiss on her forehead, and proceeded to place her body into the grave he had made. Feeling brokenhearted he began covering her body with dirt until it reached the level of the ground.

"Goodbye Ginger", Daryous said softly as he threw the last of the dirt on the grave and started to walk away.

He wondered how it had come to this. That the human race was doomed, and now he was left all alone. He sat down by a nearby tree and wished this had all been a dream. He couldn't remember a time before this monster had come. He wondered how much longer he had to live. While he sat there wondering what to do next, the ground began to rumble. He looked over at Ginger's grave and realized the rumbling noise was coming from in there. He watched and the ground seemed to rise from inside the grave.

Daryous gasped "Impossible!"

Chapter Four

He looked over just in time to see Ginger coming out of her grave.

"GINGER!" Daryous yelled happily.

But Ginger didn't look right. Her skin was cracking and her hair was falling out. Her once blue eyes now seemed to be glowing red. Almost immediately, Ginger started to transform into . . .

Daryous gasped . . . "PRODOMON!"

Daryous shook his head. All he knew was his friend had just died and then turned into Prodomon right before his very eyes. I mean talk about magic!

Daryous stared in disbelief, his body slumped forward.

"How did this happen? Prodomon can change form? Where was Ginger?" All these thoughts were racing through his head as Prodomon stared at him with those razor sharp teeth, greeting him with a smile.

As he stood there watching Prodomon coming closer to him, he thought he saw a shadow move. He turned his head slightly to see a shadow dart past the trees.

"Ginger", he thought, "She's alive?"

His heart jumped for joy in his chest at the thought. He had to remain focused because Prodomon was still coming right towards him.

"How did he change form and why did he change into Ginger?" he thought.

He realized that Prodomon had more power then he had given him credit for. He must have been trying to trick him by pretending to be Ginger, knowing he would get close enough for Prodomon to try to kill him.

"Why didn't he?", Daryous's thought was interrupted by the sound of a piercing whisper.

"Pssst . . . Pssst . . . over here".

He turned to see Ginger cowering behind a pile of rocks maybe 15 feet in front of him. She was motioning him to come towards her. He looked up at Prodomon who seemed to have become distracted by her whispers. Obviously, he was trying to figure out where she was hiding. Daryous pointed to some nearby rocks, a few feet from where she stood, and motioned her to go over there. He looked back to make sure that Prodomon wasn't looking and ran to her side behind the rocks.

"What happened to you?", Daryous asked Ginger once they were settled behind the rocks.

"Well, I hit Prodomon's foot with my club which surprised him long enough for you to escape. Then I hid behind some of the rocks in the cave. Once you were safe, I tried to get away. I threw rocks towards the back of the cave to make him think someone was there. It worked but a little too well. He started to tear the cave apart, and I almost got crushed. I had to curl up in a fetal position while the rest of the cave came down around me. Almost all of it missed me. Unfortunately, one rock got lucky and hit me on the head. I woke up to find I was alone in the cave with blood in my hair, and Prodomon was gone. Somehow he didn't see me. Maybe his eyesight is not very good?", Ginger explained.

"Well that explains where you were last night", Daryous said while trying to take in all the information she had just given him.

"Look!" said Ginger. "Prodomon is leaving. I guess we lost him."

"Yeah I guess you might have been right about his eyesight after all. This might be to our advantage. If he does have a blind spot of some sort, then it may be easier for us to sneak up on him and kill him", Daryous said excitedly.

"Maybe they had finally caught a break", Daryous thought. At least now they could get close to him without getting eaten. His thoughts were interrupted by Ginger.

"It's getting late. Maybe we should get some rest. It's been a long day", Ginger said while rubbing her eyes.

CHAPTER FIVE

THEY DECIDED TO lay down in the meadows behind the rocks. They hoped that the rocks would offer shelter from them being seen. The sun was just starting to set. It looked like it was falling behind the mountain. The sky was brilliantly lit with hues of purple, orange and red. As Daryous watched the sun set and the sky become dark, he noticed all the stars. They were all shining like glittering diamonds. It was so brilliantly lit up he could probably see the big dipper and the small dipper if he looked hard enough. Soon he fell asleep. Ginger fell asleep soon after. Suddenly she awoke. She got up and realized that she was standing on a cloud. She wasn't sure if she was still dreaming as she started to walk through a thick cloud in front of her. She noticed that the sky around her was the same colors as before. purple, orange and red. The same ones that she saw a few moments ago.

"Thats strange?" Ginger said.

She started to see a person, and he was sitting on a throne. He was at least 12 feet tall, she thought. He had hair of gold. He was dressed in a white robe and had a wreath of gold leaves on top of his head. Above the throne, it said in big bold letters, "XENON—HOLDER OF LIGHTNING, RULER OF THE SKY, HEAD LORD OF THE GODS".

"W . . . what?" Ginger stammered. Her eyes looked as if she had just seen a Giganotosaurus walk by.

Xenon started to speak. His eyes glowed gold as he spoke. It was almost like lightning was flashing from his eyes.

"GINGER", he said in a low and bold voice, "If you succeed in destroying Prodomon, I will blow up your world and I will leave you on earth!"

"Why do you hate us? What did we do to you that was so wrong that you feel you must kill the entire human race? There has to be something that we can do to change your mind?", Ginger questioned. She could fecl herself shaking with fear at the sight of him looming down on her. His eyes glowed gold and he smiled.

Xenon started to speak but it was very faint. All she could hear him say was "There is . . ." and something about Daryous. Everything else began to fade.

"What?" Ginger said putting her hand to her ear, but the vision started to get blurry, and then everything went black!

Chapter Six

"AHHHHH!". GINGER WOKE up yelling. She looked around and realized she was still in the meadows.

"Oh, it was all a dream", she said trying to catch her breath. Her heart thumping in her chest so loud she swore Daryous could hear it.

"But it wasn't just a normal dream. It was a warning", Ginger said aloud to herself. That thought brought tears to her eyes. She turned to find Daryous sleeping so calmly. His blond hair lying perfectly in the grass as if it had been molded that way. Even his clothes, which were now tattered, seemed to fit in perfectly with the grassy meadows. He looked so peaceful lying there, which actually started to make her mad, especially after what she just went through.

"Daryous, wake up!" she screamed loudly in his ear.

Daryous jumped up, scared to death and ready to fight.

"WHAT . . . WHAT DO YOU WANT! CAN'T YOU SEE I'M TRYING TO GET SOME SLEEP HERE? WHY ARE YOU SCREAMING IN MY EAR?" Daryous leaned and yelled in Ginger's face.

Ginger felt sorry for scaring him to death but she couldn't let him know that. She knew she had to keep her game face on. This was important and he needed to listen.

"Listen Mr. Sassy Pants, one . . . its morning Bozo, two . . . get up lazy and three. IT'S AN EMERGENCY OK!" Ginger exclaimed.

"So what is it anyways?" Daryous growled.

"The gods sent me a message in my dreams saying that if we kill Prodomon they'll blow up the world!", Ginger explained.

"What?" Daryous asked.

"Exactly what I said. But Xenon did say that there may be a way to stop him from destroying the world if we do manage to kill Prodomon", Ginger explained.

"So what was it? How do we stop the gods from destroying the world?" Daryous asked.

"Unfortunately, my dream got fuzzy after he said that so I don't know. All I know is that it has something to do with you", Ginger replied.

"Why would you say that?", Daryous asked.

"Because I heard him say, "there is" and then something about you. I guess he expects us to figure that out on our own ", Ginger stated.

"Oh, great! That will be easy", Daryous laughed, shaking the leaves from his blond hair.

"What should we do now? Do we still try to kill him or . . . ?", Ginger was interrupted by the sound of rumbling coming from the ground beneath her.

"What is that?", she asked Daryous.

Just then the trees began to seperate and fall, and the ground start to shake in a rhythmic pattern. A dark shadow began to emerge just beyond the rocks of the cave.

"He's back." Daryous stated, and he looked up to see Prodomon standing there, holding a hammer about to crush Ginger. Daryous grabbed for Ginger just as the hammer started to come down.

Chapter Seven

"Dear God, now he has weapons!", cried Daryous as he swept Ginger out of the hammers path. The hammer went crashing down . . . THUD!

Prodomon yelled in anger and the hammer missed them.

"Well, now what are we going to do?", Ginger asked Daryous as they ran for the rocks on higher ground to hide.

Before Daryous could answer, the sky opened up and started to rain. Lightening struck the tree nearby and branches started to fall off.

"Oh great . . . like we needed another challenge", Daryous sighed.

Daryous looked at Ginger's frightened expression and a wave of rage fell over him. Suddenly, he grabbed the biggest fallen tree branch that he could hold and started running towards Prodomon. As he ran, he lifted the tree branch high over his head ready for a fight.

Ginger screamed, "Daryous, No!!!"

He ignored Ginger's screams to turn back and headed full steam ready to beat Prodomon unconscious, if he could. The rain was beating so hard he could not see anything in front of him. All of a sudden lightning hit the ground right between him and Prodomon, knocking Daryous off his feet. Prodomon fell backwards as well. Daryous sat dazed on the ground. He could faintly hear Ginger still screaming for him.

"Was that a sign from the gods?", he thought. He knew Ginger had said the man in her dreams was Xenon—Master of the Sky and Holder of Lightning. "If this was not the way he was allowed to be destroyed, what was?" he thought.

"What do you want from me? What do I have to do to save the human race?", Daryous yelled up at the sky hoping that Xenon was listening.

The clouds began to move away from each other enough where the rain stopped falling. A rainbow shined through right into the lake that was beyond the hill. Daryous could faintly see it.

"Maybe he can't swim? Maybe that's the only way to destroy him? Is that what this message was suppose to be?", Daryous wondered to himself.

All at once, the rain stopped. Daryous began to wipe the water off of his face and shake his hair. He smoothed his blond hair back so that his bangs were no longer in his eyes. As he began to get up off the ground, he heard Ginger start screaming again.

"Daryous look up now!", she screamed as loud as she could.

Daryous looked up to see that Prodomon had come out of his daze and was walking towards him with intense rage in his eye holding his huge metal hammer.

"I kill you now puny human!", Prodomon smiled and ran towards Daryous as fast as he could.

CHAPTER EIGHT

DARYOUS STARED IN awe, his jaw dropped.

"Did he just speak?", he thought.

"What are you standing around for? RUN!", Ginger yelled from behind the rocks.

Daryous, realizing he was about to get trampled, started running to Ginger. He jumped behind the rocks quickly, hoping that Prodomon didn't see which way he went.

"So what's the plan? ", asked Ginger while trying to keep one eye on Prodomon's whereabouts at the same time.

"I think I found out a way to kill Prodomon. I'll make him chase me into the deep part of the lake. I will swim around to get him to come in. As soon as he enters the deep water, I will swim to shore and hopefully he will drown", explained Daryous.

"What makes you think that will work, and how do we know that the gods will not destroy Earth?", Ginger asked.

"I don't know for sure, but when the rainbow appeared over the lake, it came to me. Maybe that's what Xenon was trying to tell you in your dream. Either way it's worth a try. We can't live in fear of him forever. We need to take a stand. Are you with me?", Daryous asked Ginger.

Her eyes were as wide as can be. He knew all his hopes rested on her being part of this plan. He could not do this alone. She would need to be his eyes when he was swimming to make sure Prodomon didn't get to him so easily. He also hoped that this monster couldn't swim.

Ginger took a deep breath and said, "Ok, I'm with you. Now what?"

"Just wait here a minute. I'm going to see where he went", Daryous said as he realized Prodomon was no where around them, or so he thought.

Behind him came a growl. Prodomon had found their hiding place. He smiled. His razor sharp teeth grinding against each other.

CHAPTER NINE

"Run!", screamed Ginger as she grabbed Daryous's arm.

Daryous and Ginger ran over the hill towards the lake with Prodomon right behind them. It seemed like it was taking forever. Every time Prodomon got too close, they had to run and hide so they wouldn't get smashed by his hammer.

"How exactly are we going to do this?", asked Ginger while they were hiding behind some big rocks up on the hilltop. Prodomon was nearby, breaking trees down with his hammer, looking for them.

"I need him to follow me into the lake. Then, once he has waded out into the deep water, I will need you to distract him long enough for me to get out. I am going to have to stay somewhat close to him in order for him to see me. If something goes wrong, I want you to leave me and run for cover. Do you understand?", Daryous asked.

"Ok, I understand", Ginger replied sadly.

She didn't want to lose her only friend in this world. She was scared of being alone. After all, she was only a kid. At least that's how she felt. Truthfully, she wasn't sure anymore how old she was but she knew she had to be around 16 years old or so. Daryous always seemed older. She had guessed he was in his twenties or so. She had always admired him, even now in what might be his last hours on Earth.

"What if he doesn't see me because of his bad eyesight?", Ginger asked.

"Then you run and hide and hope he doesn't survive", Daryous replied with a sly smile on his face.

While Prodomon was smashing a nearby tree, Daryous grabbed Ginger's arm and then began running towards the lake again. Prodomon saw them and began to run. The ground shook more and more violently the closer he got to them. Finally they arrived at the beach. Daryous turned to Ginger.

"Ok, go hide and wait for my signal. Then when I signal you, run to the beach and start screaming to get his attention. I will do the rest", Daryous explained.

"Ok, one problem—what is the signal? You forgot to show me that", Ginger stated sarcastically. She smiled at him, her blue eyes seemed to sparkle.

"I will wave my arms like this", Daryous replied while waving his arms over his head. "Once I do that, just make a lot of noise. Hopefully Prodomon will look at you, and I can swim for shore without him noticing. By then the water should be over his head, and he will be so heavy that he will sink."

"Got it ", replied Ginger.

Just as Ginger was talking, the ground began to rumble even louder. Prodomon was getting very close. Just then, Daryous gave a thumbs up at Ginger and ran in the water. Prodomon chased after Daryous down the beach and into the cool blue water. Daryous started to swim as fast as he could towards the deepest part of the lake. Prodomon followed keeping pace with Daryous. Soon the water was rising over Prodomon's head. Daryous stopped and turned around to look at Ginger who was standing on the beach watching. Daryous began frantically waiving his arms at Ginger. Ginger then started to yell and smacking two rocks together that she had found on the beach. Prodomon turned to look at her. He began to go under water, his arms swinging above. Daryous immediately started to swim towards her as fast as he could. All of a sudden Daryous was pulled underwater. Prodomon had grabbed his left foot and dragged him under. Ginger could only watch in horror as Daryous was drowning. Daryous was under the water kicking as hard as he could, fighting for survival. Daryous managed a good kick with his right foot right into Prodomon's eye. Prodomon released his foot immediately. Ginger gasped as Daryous came up from under the water and began swimming towards her again. Finally he reached the shore. He lay on the beach trying to catch his breath while Ginger sat by him asking him if he was ok. As they sat on the beach, they watched

Prodomon drown. Lots of bubbles came up from under the water and then just stopped.

"Is it over?", Ginger asked Daryous "Are we finally free?"

Before Daryous could answer, waves started to appear on the water. Bubbles and steam began to rise out of the blue water and into the bright sunlight. As the waves got bigger and bigger, the steam and bubbles got more violent looking like a volcano was about to explode. Just then fins appeared out of the water heading towards the beach. As it slowly approached them Daryous could see two red eyes coming up out of the water. Attached to it was the fins and the rest of the creature.

"*No, it's not over*", Daryous turned and said to Ginger as the creature began to ride the waves toward them at a rapid speed.

What's waiting next for Daryous and Ginger as they go on a hazardous, dangerous monster infested journey. *Join them in The Curse of the Two Headed Bloodcurdling Diseased Dragonfish.* Coming soon.